Halloween Alphabet

An Amazing ABC's Backwards Book!

By Riley Weber

RileyWeberArt.com

Get ready for the Halloween Alphabet!
A is for….Wait!… No it's Halloween,
We're going to do it backwards, like we should.

Z is for those zig-zagging zombies

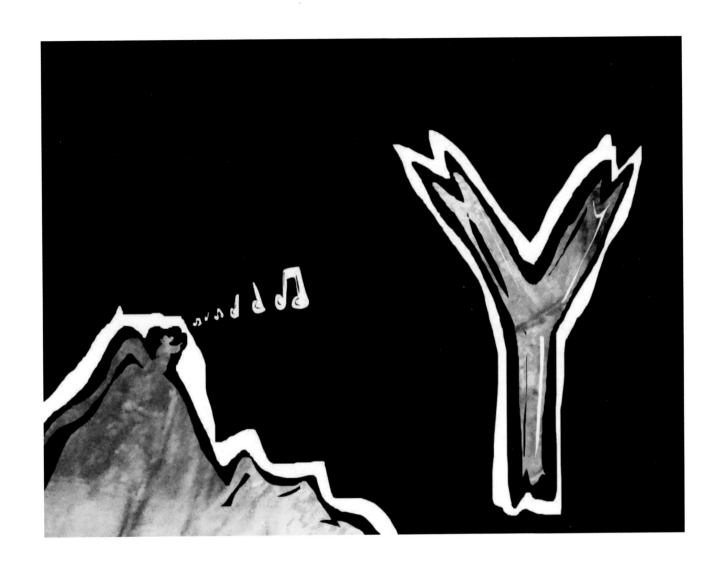

Y is for the youthful yodeling Yoda's

X is for an x-ray of a skeleton

W is for wicked weary witches

V is for vain vaunting vampires
(I vant to eat your candy)

U is for uncanny UFO's

T is for teenage trick-or-treaters

S is for the scary screams

R is for raunchy rancid recipes

Q is for quietly quilting
(with your porch light off, cricket)

P is for pick'n parties at the pumpkin patch
(I think I found a good one)

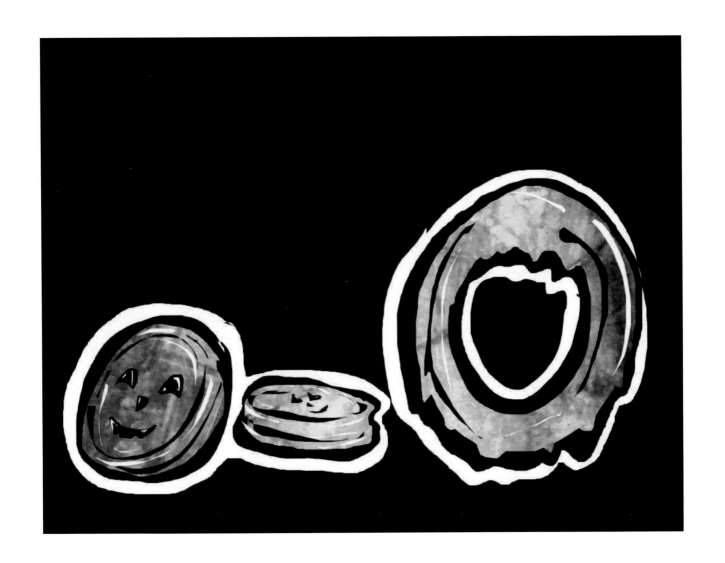

O is for orange filled Oreos
(In October)

N is for the nomads on a Nimbus 2000
(Slow down Harry!)

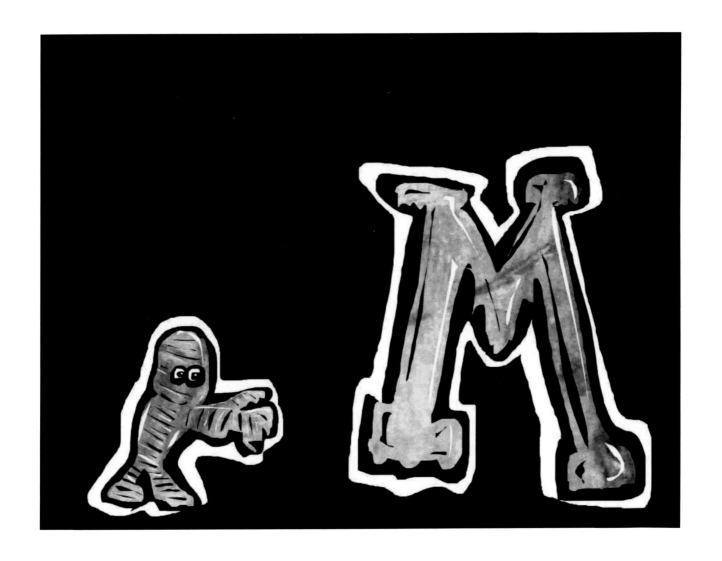

M is for mumbling moaning mummies

L is for life-like monsters

K is kegs of root beer n' karaoke
(I got the next song, give me the mic!)

J is for jumping jack-o-lanterns

I is for impressive and incredible costumes

H is for the haunted house
(I will not go in that place!)

G is for ghosts, ghouls, and goblins

F is for freaky Frankenstein

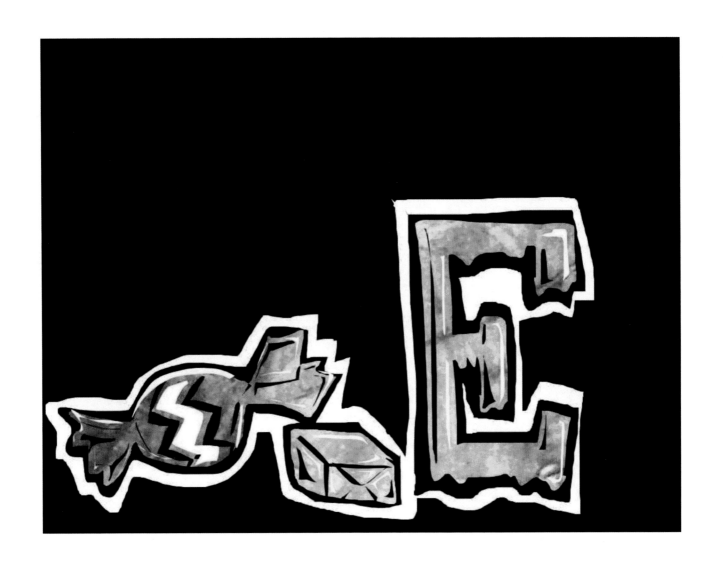

E is for edible delights
(Eat your candy!)

D is for a dark drooling Dracula

C is for the creepy crawlies in the cemetery

B is for black cats, big-ol'-bats, bobbing for apples in big ol vats

A is for AAAAHHHHHHH!!!!!!

More fun books for kids by Riley Weber…

Funny Jokes
(Silly short jokes that are colorfully illustrated for kids)

Knock Knock Jokes
(Knock knock jokes like you've never seen before. Illustrated. Every one of them. 50 plus pages of funny knock knock jokes for kids)

Tongue Twisters
(50 new and challenging tongue twisters to give your tongue some exercises. These are like push-ups for the tongue. Every one features a silly cartoony illustration)

Easter Jokes for Kids
(Hilarious Jokes for kids that will 'crack' you up like an Easter egg. Short silly illustrated jokes guaranteed to put a smile on you and the kid's faces.)

Christmas Jokes
(Funny illustrated jokes about Santa, snowmen, Christmas trees, Yeti's, and much more)

Thanksgiving Jokes
(A visual jokes book for kids with a 'corny'-copia full of jokes.)

Valentines Riddles
(Fun illustrated collection of Valentines riddles to entertain and stimulate the imagination of children, bringing smiles to their faces)

Three Little Pigs
(Will the big bad wolf beat down the pigs houses once and for all? Find out within)

Made in the USA
Middletown, DE
15 October 2021